BEAR of My HEART

Joanne Ryder · Illustrated by Margie Moore

Simon & Schuster Books for Young Readers

New York   London   Toronto   Sydney

SIMON & SCHUSTER BOOKS FOR YOUNG READERS
An imprint of Simon & Schuster Children's Publishing Division
1230 Avenue of the Americas, New York, New York 10020
Text copyright © 2007 by Joanne Ryder
Illustrations copyright © 2007 by Margie Moore
SIMON & SCHUSTER BOOKS FOR YOUNG READERS is a trademark of Simon & Schuster, Inc.
Book design by Lucy Ruth Cummins
The text for this book is set in Aunt Mildred.
The illustrations for this book are rendered in watercolor.
Manufactured in China
4 6 8 10 9 7 5 3
Library of Congress Cataloging-in-Publication Data
Ryder, Joanne.
Bear of my heart / Joanne Ryder ; illustrated by Margie Moore.— 1st ed.
p. cm.
Summary: A mama bear tells her baby how she will always love him.
ISBN-13: 978-0-689-85947-2
ISBN-10: 0-689-85947-3
[1. Mother and child—Fiction. 2. Bears—Fiction. 3. Stories in rhyme.] I. Moore, Margie, ill. II. Title.
PZ8.3.R9595Bea 2006
[E]—dc22   2005011491

To Larry, the bear of my heart—J. R.
For Maya, Tiff, and Belle—M. M.

There are so many bears in the world, dear,

but there's no other one that will do.

You are the bear of my heart, dear,
and I am the one who loves you.

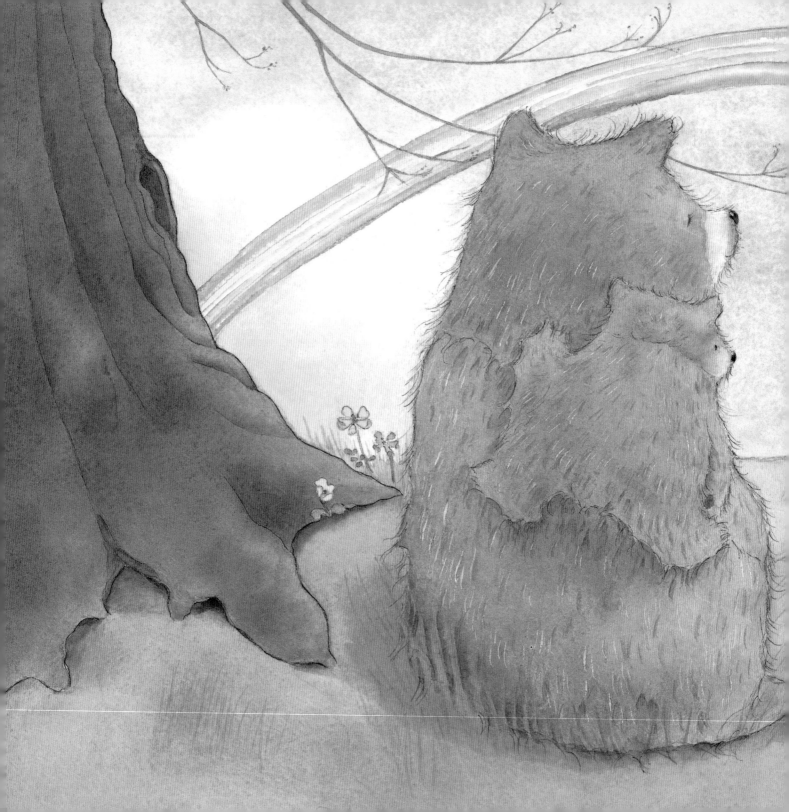

I have so many stories to tell you.
I know wonderful places to see.

And because we can see them together,
they'll be nicer for you and for me.

Let's race in the sun and be happy.

Let's splash in the stream and drip dry.

Let's roll down a hill and be silly.

Let's lie and watch clouds drifting by.

Let's sit nose to nose and share secrets.
Let's wish on a star, eyes shut tight.

Let's whisper our dreams in the darkness.
Let's snuggle together at night.

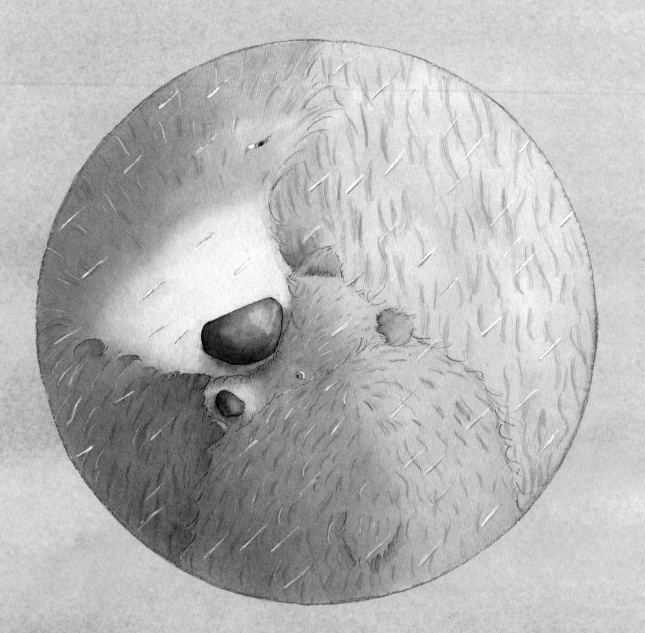

If you need me, I'll be there beside you.

If you're lonely, I'll hug you awhile.

If you're lost, I will be there to guide you.

If you're sad, I won't quit till you smile.

Paw in paw, we will greet every morning.

Paw in paw, we will meet every day.

You are the bear of my heart, dear,
and nothing can take that away.

No matter how big you may grow, dear,
or whether we're near or apart,

I will love you forever and ever,
for YOU are the bear of my heart.